My hand shot up in an instant. I knew what Mrs. Gibson was going to say, and I was going to be the first to volunteer. She was about to ask for a volunteer to sit out. You know, not to be in the dance. I jumped up and down with my hand in the air.

"Raymond, you didn't let me finish," she said.

"I know, but whatever it is, I'll do it," I said.

"Great, that's very nice of you, Raymond. It will help us all out," she said. "Okay, since we have one extra boy, Raymond has volunteered to be my partner. Raymond and I will be teaching you the dance up here in front."

WHAT?! I screamed inside my head. *Dance with the teacher?*

OTHER BOOKS YOU MAY ENJOY

Encyclopedia Brown, Boy Detective #1	Donald J. Sobol
Encyclopedia Brown and the Case of the Secret Pitch #2	Donald J. Sobol
Encyclopedia Brown Finds the Clues #3	Donald J. Sobol
Hank the Cowdog #1: The Original Adventures of Hank the Cowdog	John R. Erickson
Hank the Cowdog #2: The Further Adventures of Hank the Cowdog	John R. Erickson
Horrible Harry and the Ant Invasion	Suzy Kline
Horrible Harry and the Dungeon	Suzy Kline
Horrible Harry and the Green Slime	Suzy Kline
Raymond and Graham Rule the School	Mike Knudson & Steve Wilkinson
The Time Warp Trio #1: The Knights of the Kitchen Table	Jon Scieszka
The Time Warp Trio #2: The Not-So-Jolly Roger	Jon Scieszka
The Time Warp Trio #3: The Good, the Bad, and the Goofy	Jon Scieszka
Vet Volunteers #1: Fight for Life	Laurie Halse Anderson
Vet Volunteers #2: Homeless	Laurie Halse Anderson

DANCING DUDES

BY **Mike Knudson**

ILLUSTRATED BY
Stacy Curtis

PUFFIN BOOKS
An Imprint of Penguin Group (USA) Inc.

PUFFIN BOOKS
Published by the Penguin Group
Penguin Young Readers Group, 345 Hudson Street, New York, New York 10014, U.S.A.
Penguin Group (Canada), 90 Eglinton Avenue East, Suite 700,
Toronto, Ontario, Canada M4P 2Y3 (a division of Pearson Penguin Canada Inc.)
Penguin Books Ltd, 80 Strand, London WC2R 0RL, England
Penguin Ireland, 25 St Stephen's Green, Dublin 2, Ireland (a division of Penguin Books Ltd)
Penguin Group (Australia), 250 Camberwell Road, Camberwell, Victoria 3124, Australia
(a division of Pearson Australia Group Pty Ltd)
Penguin Books India Pvt Ltd, 11 Community Centre,
Panchsheel Park, New Delhi - 110 017, India
Penguin Group (NZ), 67 Apollo Drive, Rosedale, North Shore 0632, New Zealand
(a division of Pearson New Zealand Ltd.)
Penguin Books (South Africa) (Pty) Ltd, 24 Sturdee Avenue,
Rosebank, Johannesburg 2196, South Africa

Registered Offices: Penguin Books Ltd, 80 Strand, London WC2R 0RL, England

First published in the United States of America by Banjo Books in a slightly different form, 2007
First published by Viking, a division of Penguin Young Readers Group, 2008
Published by Puffin Books, a division of Penguin Young Readers Group, 2010

3 5 7 9 10 8 6 4 2

THE LIBRARY OF CONGRESS HAS CATALOGED THE VIKING EDITION AS FOLLOWS:
Knudson, Mike.
Raymond and Graham, dancing dudes / by Mike Knudson ; illustrated by Stacy Curtis.
p. cm.
Summary: Fourth-grade best friends Raymond and Graham write Valentine poems, perform a
hoedown, and learn how to be men.
ISBN: 978-0-670-01102-5 (hc)
[1. Schools—Fiction. 2. Maturation (Psychology)—Fiction. 3. Valentine's Day—Fiction.
4. Best friends—Fiction. 5. Friendship—Fiction.] I. Curtis, Stacy, ill. II. Title.
PZ7.K7836Raq 2008 [Fic]—dc22 2008008383

Puffin Books ISBN 978-0-14-241508-5

Printed in the United States of America

Set in Chaparral MM
Book design by Jim Hoover

For Michael, Alex, Maddie, Adam, and Abbie—all my dancing dudes —M.K.

For Brandon Kitchens —S.C.

Prologue

YOU CAN BE called a lot of things in fourth grade. You can be called a wimp, a dork, and even a weenie and still survive. But there's one thing you never want to be called: a baby. It's a word so humiliating it could ruin your whole life, or at least your fourth-grade life. Fortunately for Graham and me, we had successfully avoided it all year so far. But in the fourth grade, everything can change in a matter of seconds. . . .

1

Corn Dogs and Crybabies

"OKAY, STUDENTS. Let's put away our math books," Mrs. Gibson said. I wondered what was going on. We usually did math all the way until lunchtime.

Mrs. Gibson stood up and adjusted her huge glasses higher on her wrinkly nose. Then she picked up an old-looking book from her desk, opened it, and began reading.

"'How do I love thee? Let me count the ways,'" she read. Then she paused and lowered her book, looking around the class. She looked me straight in the eye. I turned away quickly. It felt weird having an old lady say that and then look right at me.

She continued reading. It was a poem all about love and mushy stuff. Finally, she finished and closed the book.

"Why do you think I read that poem to you?" she asked.

"Because you're a great reader and a great teacher and a great . . ." Lizzy said, trying to think of as many "great" things as possible. I can't stand Lizzy. Not only is she the biggest teacher's pet, but just looking at her annoys me. I mean, that bouncy curly hair, the big bow on her head, and that scrunched-up, snooty look on her face—everything about her bugs me.

"No, Lizzy," Mrs. Gibson answered. "Why would I be reading this poem to you *at this time of year*? You all know what holiday is coming up on Thursday," she said with a long, wrinkly smile.

"Christmas!" David yelled out, laughing.

Mrs. Gibson's smile turned quickly to a frown. "David, remind me to move your desk up here by mine this afternoon," she said. "Now who can *really* tell me why I read that poem to you?"

Everyone raised their hand. But no one was quicker than Graham. His hand shot up like a rocket, his fingers wiggling all over the place trying to get picked. Graham is my best friend. We do everything together. If he wasn't a lot shorter than I am and didn't have all those freckles and red hair, I bet people would think we were brothers.

"Graham," Mrs. Gibson said.

"Because it's almost Valentine's Day, the holiday of *love*," he said, making his eyebrows move up and down, up and down. Everyone laughed, including Mrs. Gibson. I could tell Graham was happy to have his eyebrow back after accidentally shaving it off earlier this year. It would have looked weird with only one eyebrow moving up and down.

"That's right, Graham, and I'm glad you are so enthusiastic about Valentine's Day," Mrs. Gibson answered with a little chuckle. I was laughing, too, when all of a sudden I felt a slug to my arm.

"Ouch! What was that for?" I turned to David. It

hurt so bad I almost started to cry. In fact, I had to hurry and wipe away a tear.

"That's for your friend Graham doing that stupid thing with his eyebrows." David could always think of a reason for punching me. "Hey, you're crying!" he said, sticking his fat face in front of mine.

"I am not!"

"Are too! You're such a baby!" he said. Heidi sat in front of me, and I'm sure she heard the whole thing. I didn't want her to think I was a baby. I kind of liked her . . . you know, like a girlfriend. I thought she might like me, too, but I wasn't sure.

I guess Mrs. Gibson heard the whole thing, too.

"David, why don't you move your desk up here by mine right now, and you can keep it there the rest of the week," she said.

"Baby!" David whispered as he got up to move his desk.

"I am *not* a baby," I snapped back. *Besides,* I thought to myself, *who wouldn't cry if they got slugged in the arm that hard?* David's the biggest kid in our school . . . and the meanest. Once in the second grade, he was picking on Graham. I don't know what got into me, but for some reason I had to go and open my big mouth. "Hey, why don't you pick on someone your own size?" I yelled.

David turned from Graham and walked over to me. "Fine, how about you?" Then he slugged me in the arm. He's been hitting me in the arm ever since. I learned quickly that if you punch him back, he just hits you again, but harder. So until I get really huge one day and can hit harder than he can, I just live with the daily slug.

Mrs. Gibson continued talking as David dragged his desk to the front of the room. "I just read to you a famous poem by Elizabeth Barrett Browning. With Valentine's Day this week, I thought it would be a good idea to write some poems of our own. Doesn't that sound like fun?"

"I think it sounds like fun, Mrs. Gibson," Lizzy said. "And I really—"

"Thank you Lizzy, that's enough. Everyone, please make sure your books are in your desk, and you may line up for lunch." We all ran up to the doorway and formed a line. I stood next to Graham, as usual.

We walked down the hall together wondering what they were serving for lunch. We always tried to guess by the smell in the hall.

I took a big whiff. "I say it's chicken nuggets."

"No way," Graham said. "It's definitely hamburgers." Graham was usually right. He buys school lunch every day, and I bring mine from home. The only lunchroom smell I knew for sure was fish sticks. I hate fish. Just the smell of it makes me lose my appetite. One time, on one of those rare, special occasions when Mom packed a Twinkie in my lunch, the smell of fish sticks was so strong I couldn't even eat it. I was so mad. I get a Twinkie or a Ding Dong, like, maybe once a year or less. Anyway, I knew today was definitely not a fish-stick day.

We walked into the lunchroom and quickly looked around at everyone's trays. Corn dogs. We were both wrong. Graham stood in line while I saved us a place at a table. I sat down across from Heidi and Diane.

"Hi, Raymond, are you up for a game of Who Has the Best Sandwich?" Heidi said. One thing I like about Heidi is how funny she is. She's one of the only girls who can really make me laugh. She's like the opposite of Lizzy.

"I'll go first," Diane blurted out, digging into her lunch sack. She pulled out a bologna, lettuce, and cheese sandwich. "Top that," she proudly stated.

"Hmmm," Heidi said, taking a close look at the bread. "Whole wheat bread. I don't know if you can win with that."

Diane took a big bite. "What do you mean? It tastes good, and it's good for you," she said with a mouth full of bologna. Just then Graham sat down.

"What do you think, Graham? Can whole wheat bread win for best sandwich?" Diane asked, chewing and talking at the same time.

"Ooh, gross. Didn't your mom ever teach you to eat with your mouth closed?" Graham answered. "And the answer is *no*. Health food can never win a best-food contest."

Diane didn't seem to mind that nobody agreed with her. She took another big bite.

"Now *this* is sandwich perfection," Heidi announced, showing off a peanut butter and jelly sandwich on white bread with the crusts cut off. We all looked in awe. Her sandwich was every kid's dream. My mom never cut the crusts off. In fact, my mom would even use the end piece of the bread for one of my slices. You know, the piece that is all crust.

"Your turn, Raymond," Diane said.

"Yeah, I'm rooting for you," Graham said.

"All right, all right." I reached in and pulled out my sandwich. It was wrapped in tinfoil. We must have been out of sandwich bags.

"Tinfoil?" Diane laughed.

Carefully, I opened the foil and exposed a sorry-looking sandwich with a bite already taken out of it and jelly soaking through the bread. I don't know why my mom insists on taking a bite out of my sandwich when she makes my lunch. It's so humiliating.

"Okay," Heidi said. "We'll let you off the hook for the tinfoil. But bringing a used sandwich just won't cut it." Everyone laughed. "And let me give you a little advice on the jelly." She pulled apart her bread. "See, if you put peanut butter on both sides of the bread, the jelly won't soak through."

"Whoa, I never thought of that," I said. Her mom must be some kind of professional sandwich maker.

"So, did you guys hear that our class is going to do a dance instead of a song for the fourth-grade show?" Graham whispered, stretching his head to the middle of the table. "My mom said she heard it from someone on the PTA."

"No way," Diane said. "I don't believe you. It's always a singing program." She usually knew more about stuff than Graham. We all leaned back like we believed her instead of Graham.

"Okay, suit yourself. You'll see," Graham said confidently.

I looked up at Mrs. Gibson, who was by the lunch-room door talking to Mr. Worley, our principal.

"I hope Mrs. Gibson forgets about writing poems this afternoon," I said. "I don't think I could write one."

"What? Everyone can write poems. They're easy," Graham said. "Take this corn dog, for example." Graham held up his corn dog high in the air in front of him.

O my corn dog, how do I love thee, let me count the ways.
Your tasty shell of golden brown makes me happy all the days. . . .

Then he dipped his corn dog in some ketchup and took a big bite. *"Yuck!"* he said, spitting it out onto his tray. "This is disgusting! It's not even warm!"

"Wow, that was beautiful," Diane joked.

"Especially that last line—'*Yuck!*'" Heidi added.

We finished eating, and Graham and I spent the rest of lunch recess playing tetherball. I hit the ball high above Graham's head. He jumped up but missed it by a mile. I slapped it again and in no time at all it was completely wrapped around the pole.

"I'm too short for this game," Graham complained, unraveling the rope from the pole.

"No you're not. I'm just too good," I said. Just then the ball swung around and hit me in the head.

"Ouch!" I said. "I wasn't ready."

"Aw, don't be a baby," Graham said. There was that word again. First David, and now Graham.

"I am *not* a baby!" I yelled, grabbing the ball.

"Hey, relax. I didn't mean anything," he said.

"It's just that . . . well, my sister always calls me a baby, and today David called me a baby and it seemed like he really meant it. And now you, my best friend. I'm just worried that everyone thinks I'm a baby. I mean, we're in the fourth grade. What if Heidi thinks I'm a baby? Do you think there's any way a girl would like someone who everyone thinks is a baby?"

"Of course not. Girls like manly guys. Why did David call you a baby, anyway?" he asked as he tried to climb up the tetherball pole.

"Because when he hit me in class today, it really

hurt. He thought I was crying and called me a baby," I said.

"Why did he think you were crying?"

"I don't know, probably because I had some water in my eyes and I wiped it away," I said.

"What? You mean a tear?" Graham said. He immediately jumped down from the pole and looked me in the eye.

"Well, I guess so," I said. "But it was just that it hurt and—"

"Whoa, hold on, Raymond," Graham said, grabbing my shoulders. "I hate to say this, but you can't cry when you're in fourth grade. You just can't. If you want people to think you're a man and not a baby, that is the first rule."

"The first rule?" I said. "I've never heard of any rules about being a man."

Graham shook his head and put his hands on his hips. "Are you kidding me? Everyone knows there are certain rules of what you can and can't do."

I stood there wondering why my dad had never taught me these *manly* rules. "No one ever told me," I said, getting kind of mad. "I mean, of course I never want anyone to see me cry, but I didn't think that if I accidentally let one measly tear fall out of my eye it would mean that I'm a baby."

"Unfortunately, it does," Graham said. "Take it from me, if you really want to be a man, you've got to learn that there are certain things you *have* to do and other things you can *never* do."

I stood there wishing that when you got to the fourth grade, you would get some instructions on how to stop being a baby and become a man.

"Come on, it's easy," Graham said. "Just try to act like me. Hey, that's it! I can teach you what you need to do to be a man. I'll be your coach. Yeah, I'll be your manly coach."

"You?" I said, looking down at Graham. He was a lot shorter than me and had a big ketchup stain on the front of his superhero T-shirt from his corn dog. He didn't exactly look too manly. "Wouldn't someone else be better? Like someone who's more of a . . . you know . . . man?"

"Are you serious? I can teach you tons about

being a man," he said happily. "I mean, have you ever seen me cry this year?"

I thought for a moment but couldn't remember Graham crying at all since school started. As crazy as it sounded, maybe Graham did know more about being a man than I did.

"What do you say?" he said, holding out his puny hand. I thought about it for a few more seconds, then shook his hand.

"It's a deal," I said. "You are officially my *manly coach*." I wasn't sure if Graham could really help me, but I thought it was worth a try.

"Great!" Graham said. Recess was almost over, so we headed toward the door. "Hey, here's your first lesson. Go up and hold the door open for those girls and say, 'After you, ladies.'"

"But—"

"No buts," Graham interrupted. "Hurry, this will be great."

I didn't want to do it, but I ran up anyway. I opened the door and waited. Lizzy and her friends walked up.

"What are you doing?" Lizzy smirked.

"Um, after you, ladies," I said.

Lizzy looked at me really weird. Then she walked in with her friends. "I'm telling on you," she said as she passed me.

"For what?" I yelled. I let the door close by itself and walked back to Graham. He was smiling and talking to himself.

"Hello, I'm Coach Graham," he said, pretending to shake someone's hand.

I snapped my fingers a couple of times in front of his face. "Hey, that didn't go so well," I said. "How about we just start with the manly rules?"

"Oh, right," Graham said. "Rule number one: *Never* cry."

"Yeah, I figured that out. So what's rule number two?" I asked.

"It's, um, give me a second," Graham said. He thought for a minute or two as we walked back to class. "I'll tell you later."

Real Men
Write Poems

WE STARTED RIGHT in with the poetry. Mrs. Gibson taught us about how there are different types of poems. She said there are some that don't even rhyme. I couldn't believe that. How could it be poetry if it didn't rhyme? Anyway, we worked on them for most of the afternoon.

Our first poems had to be about our favorite foods. They were supposed to be in the shape of a diamond. The first line could only be one word, the name of our favorite food. The next line had two words to describe it. Then three words on the third line, two words on the fourth line, and the name of the food again on the last line. So in the end, your poem is written in the shape of a diamond. Here's mine. I wrote about cold cereal. I love cold cereal:

Cereal
Sugar milk
Prize inside box
Bowl spoon
Cereal

After we wrote our poems, we had to draw pictures about them. I drew myself pulling a new bike out of a box of Cap'n Crunch. Even though it would never fit, I thought it would be cool to find a bike as the prize in the box. I also thought Mrs. Gibson would like that. She always wants us to use our imaginations.

"Okay, students," Mrs. Gibson said at the end of the day. "There is one last thing I would like to go over before you leave. We will be decorating our valentine mailboxes tomorrow. You each need to bring an empty shoe box to school. I have a few boxes for those of you who cannot find one, but I won't have enough for everyone.

"Also, I want to go over the rules for our Valentine's Day celebration on Thursday. First, you must bring a valentine to put in the mailbox of every student. That means twenty-six valentines. Second, there will be no rude or distasteful comments written on your valentines. As Graham so eloquently stated, this is a holiday of love, not nastiness."

"I think this is a holiday of love, too, Mrs. Gibson," Lizzy called out. "I was thinking that first, even before Graham." Did I mention that Lizzy drives me nuts?

"I'm sure you were, Lizzy," Mrs. Gibson replied quietly without looking at her. Just then the bell rang. "See you tomorrow."

"This will be so sweet!" Graham said once we were outside. "I love Valentine's Day. I can finally write a love letter to Kelly without Mrs. Gibson taking it away. It's completely legal!"

"I guess you're right," I said. Graham's been in love with Kelly since the first grade. Even though she's never liked him back, he hasn't given up.

"Although," Graham continued, "maybe I shouldn't sign my name . . . you know, to be more mysterious. Maybe I'll just give her some clues in my valentine. Yeah, that's exactly what I'll do. This will be great! By the way, are you going to write a love letter to Heidi on her valentine?"

"I don't know," I said. "Maybe, if I don't sign my name. I'll have to think about it. What if she doesn't like me back?"

"Who cares if she likes you? If you like her, you should tell her in a valentine," Graham said. "Plus, you almost kissed her before Christmas vacation. Remember? If only you hadn't messed up and sneezed all over her face."

"I know, I know," I said. "You don't have to remind me."

We walked home discussing what Graham was going to write on Kelly's valentine.

"Maybe I'll write a poem," Graham said. "Girls love poems."

"How do you know?" I asked. I wondered how

Graham seemed to know so much about girls. I mean, we were only ten years old.

"What do you mean, how do I know?" Graham answered. "Didn't you see Mrs. Gibson's face when she was reading that poem about love? She had a twinkle in her eye and a big smile stretched out across her face."

"Yeah, but she's not a girl, she's an old lady," I said.

"Trust me," said Graham. "I know a lot more about girls than you do. And girls are born loving poems. In fact, that's rule number two: Real men write poems to their girlfriends. So as your manly coach, I'm giving you your next assignment: to write Heidi a poem."

He told me that if I was going to have him as my manly coach, I had to follow the rules or it wouldn't work. And since he seemed pretty confident about girls loving poetry, I figured he must be right. "Okay," I agreed. "I'll help you write one for Kelly, and I'll write one for Heidi, too." My days of being called a baby were going to be over in no time.

"We'll go to my house and start right now," Graham said excitedly.

We ran to his house and threw our backpacks on the kitchen table. We each pulled out our notebooks and pencils. I called my mom and asked if I could stay at Graham's to work on homework. Luckily she said yes.

"Great, let's do mine first," Graham said. He looked up at the ceiling with a serious expression on his face. His eyes were all squinty as he rubbed his chin. "First, I need some words that rhyme with *Kelly*."

"How about *jelly*?" I said. I love jelly, except when it's soaked into my sandwich.

"Okay, what do you think of this?" Graham said.

"Kelly, Kelly,
Like a bowl full of jelly . . ."

"Hold on," I interrupted. "Isn't that part of a Santa Claus song or something? You know, like

Santa's belly shaking when he laughs like a bowlful of jelly?"

"Oh yeah, that's right," Graham said. "I knew it sounded familiar. Then how about this?

"Kelly, Kelly,
Like some beautiful jelly,
You're much prettier than
Santa's shaking belly. . . ."

"What do you think, *hermano*?" Graham asked. He must have thought it was pretty good since he was calling me *hermano*. That means *brother* in Spanish. Usually we only use the few Spanish words we know on special occasions or when we are really happy.

I looked at Graham but I didn't know what to say, because his poem sounded kind of crazy to me. "I don't know, it seems kind of weird."

"What do you mean, weird?" Graham said. He looked sad, like I really hurt his feelings.

"Hold on, *hermano*," I said quickly. "I don't mean

the bad kind of weird. I mean, you know . . . good weird. Like when something is so good you say it's . . . weird. Like, 'Wow, that new video game is the best! It's *soooo* weird!'"

"Yeah, that's what I thought you meant," Graham said, completely happy again. "Okay, let's write your poem for Heidi."

"I don't know. We probably can't think of anything to rhyme with *Heidi*," I answered. I kind of wanted to drop the idea. Besides, I didn't want to give Heidi a poem about looking like some fat guy's belly or anything like that. But Graham wouldn't let me give up.

"Hey, this is your coach talking. If we don't write the poem, I'm going to make you do some push-ups."

"Tone it down. You're not my football coach," I said.

"Okay, sorry. But we are writing a poem for Heidi. I'm sure we can think of tons of words that rhyme with *Heidi*. Let's see . . ." he said, squinting again and mumbling. "Heidi . . . beidi . . . meidi . . . sleidi . . . Hmmm . . . Don't worry, I'll get it."

As I sat there quietly thinking of rhyming words, Graham yelled, "I've got it!" He cleared his throat and began reciting.

"Heidi, Heidi,
You are very tidy,
So please be my valentiny."

"Hmm," I said. "Tidy, eh? *You are very tidy.*" I let the line bounce around through my brain for a minute. "Heidi . . . tidy," I repeated a few more times. "You know what? I like it. It's short and to the point. And girls are way more tidy and neat than boys are. She'll probably like that I notice how tidy she is."

"Exactly," Graham said. "She'll love it. And you'll be one step closer to manliness."

"Yeah, thanks. And that didn't even seem very hard," I said. Then it came to me. "Wait a minute. We should write poems for everyone in our class. You know, not love poems, just regular poems. It'll be fun."

Graham agreed.

3

Roses Are Red, Beans Are Green

"OKAY," GRAHAM SAID. "My first poem will be for Matt Lindenheimer. Let's see . . . Lindenheimer . . . mindenheimer . . . tindenheimer . . . windenheimer . . ."

"How about you just use *Matt*?" I interrupted. This could take forever if we had to rhyme something with *Lindenheimer*.

"Yeah, *Matt*," Graham agreed. "That'll be easy. Let's see . . . how about this?

"Matt, Matt,
You're not very fat,

But you have a big brain,
So happy Valentine's Dain."

"Dain? What's a dain?" I asked.

"Come on, Raymond. That's just a poetic way of saying *day.*" Graham looked at me like I was an idiot. "You can make stuff up like that when you write a poem."

"Sweet," I said. If we could make up words, this was going to be easier than I thought. "Let me try."

"All right, why don't you do one about Lizzy," Graham suggested.

"Whoa, that will be hard," I said, "but I'll give it a shot.

"Lizzy, Lizzy,
Your hair is curly and frizzy.
Every day your face is crinklier,
Like you just smelled another stinklier.
Happy Valentine's Day."

"Great," Graham said. "And nice poetic words, too—*crinklier* and *stinklier.*"

It took all afternoon, but we each wrote a poem for every person in our class. By five o'clock, I was starving. "Hey, gotta go, Graham," I said. "I'll see you tomorrow." I stuffed my poem valentines into my backpack and ran all the way home.

I made it to my porch just as my dad pulled into the driveway.

"Hey, bud," Dad called, getting out of the car. "What have you been up to, chasing girls?"

"No. I was at Graham's writing Valentine's Day poems."

"Well, that's a sure way to catch 'em," Dad chuckled. He opened the front door for me, and I ran in.

"Mom, what's for dinner?" I yelled.

"Hi, sweetie," Mom called from the kitchen. "We're having chicken and string beans."

"Not string beans!" I yelled. Just saying it made me start to gag. They are by far the worst vegetable ever. "I'll just have the chicken."

"Sorry, sweetie, everyone has to eat some vegetables. You know that," she said.

I sat down and tried to think of some way out of it. If there is one thing Mom is serious about, it's eating your vegetables. You can't ever leave the table until you have eaten everything on your plate. Plus you don't even get to choose what you get or how much. When she sets your plate in front of you, it's already full and ready to go. Once Graham stayed over for dinner and my mom made brussels sprouts. Even though Graham said, "No thanks," Mom still loaded up his plate. I think he put them in his pocket to get rid of them when she wasn't looking. Not even visitors escape the Clean Your Plate Rule at my house.

I washed my hands and sat down at the kitchen table.

"Did you know your son's a poet?" Dad said, smiling at Mom. Just then my big sister, Geri, walked in.

"You, a poet?" she laughed. "Right."

"What did you write, Raymond?" Mom said, giving Geri a stern look.

"Graham and I wrote poems for everyone in our

class. And I have to admit, they're pretty good," I said. "Just listen to this—I'll write one about you, Mom.

"Mom, Mom,
You're so . . .
Let's see, you're so . . .

"Okay, hold on a minute," I said. I tried to think of things that rhymed with *Mom. Mom, pom, dom, gom, zom, som,* I thought to myself. Then it came to me . . . *Mother,* not *Mom. Mother* would be much easier. "Okay, here I go . . ." I said.

"Mother, Mother,
You're so . . .
You're so . . . um . . ."

"I've got one," Geri blurted out. "How about this:

"Brother, Brother,
A dork like no other,

Can't make a rhyme
For his dear old mother."

She leaned back laughing.

"Geri, that's enough," Mom said in a tone that my sister understood. Geri immediately stopped laughing and started eating. "And Raymond, I'm sure you wrote some wonderful poems today." Mom smiled at me.

Oh, great, I thought. *My mom's using her 'feel sorry for Raymond' voice.* I hated that voice. It's bad enough to have your big sister call you a dork, but to have your mom feel sorry for you for being a dork is much worse. Then a brilliant idea came to my mind. This was my ticket away from the dinner table and that pile of string beans on my plate. The best time to get away with something is when your mom feels sorry for you.

I put on a sad face and tried to make my eyes water. I even pinched myself to cry, but it didn't work. "Mom," I said in my saddest voice, rubbing my eyes, "I tried to write a good poem for you, but I guess I'm just a bad poet, like Geri said."

"Oh, honey, you're a great poet," Mom said. "Don't you worry about your sister. She's just doing what twelve-year-old sisters do."

This was working perfectly. Now for the finale. I made a sniffle noise. "Well, I finished all of my chicken, but I sort of don't feel like eating anymore. Do you think I can just go to my room and practice writing a poem for you?" I slid my chair back and started to stand up.

"Sure, sweetie," she said. Then she put her hand on my shoulder and said, "Just as soon as you finish your beans. Then you can go and write as many poems as you like."

I fell back into my chair and looked down at the pile of beans on my plate. I could feel Geri laughing at me. I stared at those beans for a long time ... a really long time. I stared at them until I was the only one left at the table. Dad cleared all of the other plates and left the kitchen. But there was absolutely no way I was going to put those beans into my mouth. I would rather stay there until I was an old man.

Maybe the beans would dry up and blow away.

As I sat there thinking about how long it would take for a bean to dry up, a thought came to mind: Maggie, our dog, eats anything. I hadn't fed her my food under the table for weeks. It used to be my regular way of finishing my dinner. I wondered why I hadn't thought of it sooner.

"Mom, I'll be right back," I said. "I just need to go to the bathroom." She set some dishes in the sink and came over to see if I was bringing my beans into the bathroom, one of my other tricks.

"Okay, sweetie, but hurry right back to finish those beans," she said.

"Of course," I said. I walked to the bathroom, waited a minute or two, and then flushed the toilet. I could see our dog down the hall in the living room.

"Come on," I whispered to Maggie. "Come on, girl. Do you want some food?" Suddenly, Maggie's ears perked up and she followed me back to the kitchen and went straight under the table. She knew the routine. I sat down and grabbed one bean and dropped it under the table to see if she would eat it. I wasn't sure if I had ever fed her a string bean. I peeked under the table, and sure enough she was eating it. I patted her head and reached for the whole pile on my plate. Mom kept her eye on me as she was cleaning up. But as soon as she opened the refrigerator to put away the butter, I grabbed the handful of beans and, without looking, reached under the table and dropped them.

I felt a little bad about not eating my vegetables, but I figured Maggie probably needed vegetables, too. Knowing that I was helping my dog eat better made me feel a little less guilty. But as I was feeling proud about helping Maggie, she crawled out from under the table and trotted toward the family room, where my dad was reading the paper. That would have been fine, but as she walked away I noticed something weird. She had a pile of string beans on her head.

Oh, no! I thought. I must have dropped some of the beans on her head instead of the floor. Before I had time to get out of my chair and into the other room, I heard my dad.

"Honey," Dad called out, "why is the dog walking around with a pile of beans on her head?"

To make a long story short, Mom had a little chat with me about the importance of eating vegetables. I also got two extra chores for the week. But in the end, if it helped me get out of eating my string beans . . . it was worth it.

4

Valentine Eggs

THE NEXT DAY after lunch, we began working on our valentine boxes. Mrs. Gibson had us move to the tables in the back of the classroom. I was at a table with Kelly, Brad, Eden, Luke, and Zach.

Mrs. Gibson put some pink, red, and white construction paper, a bunch of pink and red tissue paper, and some glue in the middle of each table. She showed us a box that a kid decorated last year. It looked pretty good. I knew right then that mine was never going to look that good. My art projects always stink.

I thought I would glue some tissue paper all

around my box first, and then I could make hearts and stuff out of the other paper and glue them on the sides. Unfortunately, I found out the hard way that you shouldn't use too much glue with tissue paper. It soaked right through and got my tissue paper all soggy. There was glue on my hands and on the table, and my tissue paper was ripping apart. I stuck it on as well as I could.

I glanced around our table to see how everyone else was doing. Zach was cutting out pink footballs and basketballs and pasting them all over his box. I looked over at Kelly, who was cutting out perfectly shaped hearts. I thought I would try that, too. I grabbed some scissors and some paper and started cutting.

"Whoa," I said, looking at the weird shape I cut out. It looked nothing like a heart. I tried a few more. They looked more like eggs. *If only this were an Easter box, it would look great,* I thought. This was harder than it looked. I peeked over at Kelly's box. It was perfect, covered in hearts of all different sizes and colors.

"Hey, Kelly," I said. "How did you make those hearts look so good? Mine look terrible."

"Oh, those are hearts?" she said. "I thought you were cutting out eggs."

"Yeah, they're *supposed* to be hearts," I said. "Do you think you could maybe cut some out for me?"

She smiled and grabbed a few pieces of paper. In no time at all, she handed me a pile of pink and white hearts.

"Wow, thanks," I said. "Hey, does anyone want to put eggs on their box? I have some extras."

"Actually," Kelly said, "I'll take them."

"What? Are you crazy?" I said. "I was just kidding."

Kelly just smiled again and took the handful of egg shapes and, in a matter of seconds, cut them into more perfectly shaped hearts.

"Wow, you *are* a heart expert," I said. I couldn't believe it. No wonder Graham likes her so much.

Mrs. Gibson clapped her hands and waited for us to quiet down. "You are all doing such wonderful work on your boxes that I hate to have you stop, but we'll have time to finish them tomorrow," she said. "So let's clean up and return to your desks. I have one more announcement to make before the bell rings."

We all cleaned up as fast as we could and ran back to our desks, wondering what it could be.

"Well, as you know, the fourth-grade recital is coming up in two weeks. Mr. Fowl's class will be singing some traditional American folk songs, and I am thrilled to announce that our class will be performing a real Western hoedown!"

We all looked at each other. Mrs. Gibson seemed much more excited than we did. "That means you will all be learning to square-dance."

I looked at Graham. He was giving Diane an *I told you so* look.

"Don't worry," Mrs. Gibson said. "You are going to have a wonderful time square-dancing. I'm sure you will all love it as much as I do. My husband and I used to have such a grand time square-dancing."

I'd never heard Mrs. Gibson mention her husband before, but my mom told me he died a long time ago. I could tell she missed him.

"Tomorrow," she said, "I will assign each of you a dance partner. That means we'll line everyone up from smallest to tallest—boys on one side, and girls on the other—so we can match you up with a dance partner close to your height."

Immediately, everyone looked around the room to see who was about their same height. The only people that I knew for sure would be paired up together were Diane and David, since they were both the tallest, and Graham and Suzy, since they were both the shortest. I hoped I would get to dance with Heidi.

Then the end-of-school bell rang, and we were all crowding through the door.

"What am I going to do, Raymond?" Graham said by the coatracks.

"What do you mean?" I asked. Graham had a serious look on his face.

"I mean how am I going to get Kelly to be my dance partner?" he asked. "This could be the moment I've waited for my entire life. Not only would I get to dance with her that night, but we'll be practicing this dance for two weeks." Graham's eyes looked crazy, and he was talking really fast.

"I never thought of it like that," I said. "But I don't know how you would do it. You and Suzy are the two shortest kids in our class. Unless you can grow overnight, you are definitely going to get matched up with Suzy tomorrow."

"You're right," Graham said. "Unless . . ." He started to smile. "Unless I wasn't at school tomorrow for the lineup. If I'm not there, Suzy will get paired up with someone else."

"That's true," I said. "But so will Kelly."

"Oh, yeah," Graham said. He thought in silence for a moment. "Maybe an idea will come to me tonight."

The next morning, Graham wasn't out on his driveway waiting for me like usual. I was about to ring his doorbell when he opened the door.

"Hey, Graham, running a little late?" I asked.

"No, just eating an extra bowl of cereal," he said.

Graham loved cereal as much as I did. "I was trying to eat as much as I could. The box said there was a toy inside, but I couldn't find it."

"That stinks," I said. "So did you figure out a way to get paired up with Kelly?"

Graham shook his head. "I couldn't think of anything," he said. "Matt is the next shortest kid, and he's still about four inches taller than me. If Suzy weren't there, it would work out great. Besides Suzy, there aren't very many short girls. Kelly's probably even the next in line."

"Yeah, you're right," I said. "At least if you don't get to dance with Kelly, you still get to give her a valentine telling her how much you like her. And she's making a great valentine box. She was sitting at my table when we made them. You'll know hers because she has a bunch of perfectly shaped hearts all over it. I mean, those hearts are *perfect*."

"Sounds like they're just as perfect as she is," Graham said in a soft voice.

Sometimes Graham says the strangest things. "Yeah, whatever you say," I said.

School started out as boring as usual. At lunch we went out and played basketball. There wasn't any snow on the playground except for some piles of slush on the sides. I stepped in one and got my shoe drenched. It was the kind of wet that I knew would stay soggy the rest of the day. Just as recess was about to end, a lady from the office came out looking for Kelly.

"What's that all about?" Graham said, staring at Kelly and the office lady.

Then Kelly called out to her friends on the playground, "I have to go—my mom's picking me up." Just as she disappeared into the school, the bell rang and recess was over.

"This is perfect!" Graham said. He had a huge smile on his face and was rubbing his hands together.

"What?" I asked. "What's so great about Kelly's mom taking her out of school?"

"Don't you get it?" Graham said. "She won't be in the lineup today for the dance partners."

"I still don't get it," I said. "It seems to me that

now you won't get paired up with Kelly for sure."

"That would be true if I were actually going to *be* here for the lineup," Graham said with an evil smile. "I think I feel something coming on, like a bad stomachache . . . if you know what I mean."

"I'm not sure I do know what you mean," I said.

"Okay, Raymond, I'll spell it out for you," Graham said, letting out a huge breath. "If Kelly is gone and I am gone, then everyone will get paired up except us. Then when we come back tomorrow, Mrs. Gibson will have no other choice than to make us partners. Now do you get it?"

"*Ooooh*, that's brilliant," I said. We both ran into class and sat down. Graham immediately made a face like David had just punched him in the stomach. Slowly, he stood up and walked over to Mrs. Gibson's desk all hunched over. I couldn't hear what he said, but it must have been good, because Mrs. Gibson got up and walked him out the door.

I couldn't believe it. I would never be able to pull that off. One, I'm a lousy actor and I never get away with anything. And two, I'm just a chicken. I was more and more convinced that Graham was definitely more manly than I was. I watched proudly as my manly coach walked down the hall.

A few minutes passed by, and Mrs. Gibson was back. "Raymond, could you bring Graham's coat to the office? He'll be going home as soon as his mother arrives," she said.

"Okay," I answered. I grabbed his coat and ran down the hall.

"Walk, please. . . ." I heard Mrs. Gibson calling from our room. I stopped running and walked the rest of the way.

Graham was sitting in a chair in the office by the fish tank.

"Graham, I can't believe you're going home. How did you do it?" I asked.

He put his hands behind his head and leaned back. "Ah, it was a cinch. I just said I felt like I was about to throw up," he said. "And it seemed like Mrs. Gibson didn't want any of that in her classroom, so she just took me straight here. By the way, I just thought of manly rule number three: A man does whatever it takes to dance with his girl."

"Yeah, well, good luck," I said. "I'll call you and tell you what happens—I've got to get back to class."

"See you, *hermano*," Graham called out in his sick voice as I left the office. I walked back to class going over the manly rules: never cry, always write poems for your girlfriend, and do whatever it takes to dance with her.

We spent the next hour working on our valentine boxes. Mine was looking much better with the hearts Kelly gave me.

"When you finish, be sure to put your names on your boxes," Mrs. Gibson said. Then she picked up Kelly's box and held it high for all of us to see. "Kelly was very creative and wrote her name in little hearts. So don't be afraid to be creative with your name as well."

Kelly's box looked great. I wished I had thought of that. Then I saw a bunch of extra tiny hearts that Kelly had cut out but hadn't used yet. Since she left with her mom, I thought I would just borrow a few and write my name in hearts, too. There weren't enough to write my whole name, so I just made a big *R* for *Raymond*.

This was turning out to be my best school project ever. Usually my art projects never look good. Last year we made clay sculptures of our heads and put them in one of those ovens that turn clay hard like a statue. I rolled a bunch of thin pieces of clay for my hair, but somehow I didn't stick them on very well and they fell off in the oven. When it came out, it looked like a crazy old bald man. I took it home and my mom actually thought it was a statue of my grandpa's head.

We worked on the boxes for a long time. I wondered if Mrs. Gibson forgot that she told us she would be assigning dance partners today. But it was like she read my mind, because just then she said, "Okay, everyone, it looks like you're all finished. Let's put your boxes down and come to the front of the room."

The moment we had all waited for was about to begin. "Boys, I need you to line up tallest to smallest," she said. We all scurried around trying to get in order. She had to switch a few people who were in the wrong spots. Then she did the same thing with the girls.

I almost jumped for joy when I turned to see Heidi lined up right next to me.

"I guess I'm stuck with you," Heidi joked.

"I guess so." I smiled. I couldn't wait to get home and tell Graham.

Then, as everything looked so perfect, something terrible happened: Kelly walked through the doorway.

"Just in time, Kelly," Mrs. Gibson said. "Come stand here next to Suzy."

Oh, no! What about Graham? I thought.

When Kelly got into the line, all the girls moved down. Suddenly, I found myself face-to-face with Lizzy. I stopped worrying about Graham and started worrying about *me*.

"Wait!" I called out. I could hear Graham reciting manly rule number three in my head: *A man does whatever it takes to dance with his girl.*

"What is it, Raymond?" Mrs. Gibson asked.

"Shouldn't I be with Heidi instead of Lizzy?" I said. Lizzy gave me a nasty look.

Mrs. Gibson glanced over. "No, I think we're fine the way we are," she said. She continued on down to the end of the line.

"All right, it looks like we've done it. And we have a perfect number of boys and girls," she said.

"Wait," I called out. "Graham is missing. That means we have one extra boy."

"Thank you, Raymond. I forgot that Graham went home," she said. "We'll take care of that tomorrow."

5

Dancing Gramps

AFTER SCHOOL, I ran to Graham's house. I rang his doorbell, hoping his mom would let me see him even though he was technically sick. Graham peeked out the window and then opened the door. I walked right in.

"Oh, man, this is bad," I started, without even saying hi.

"Hold on, Raymond, what are you talking about?" Graham asked. He had a Popsicle in his hand.

"No way, you get Popsicles, too?" I said, forgetting for a moment about the hoedown.

"Yeah, and not only that, my mom is at the store

buying me some soda pop. She says it will help my stomach." Graham smiled.

"No fair," I said.

"Hey, what were you saying about something being bad?"

"Oh, yeah, I almost forgot," I said. "Guess who walked through the door right when we were lining up for dance partners?"

"Um, how about Gordon Armstrong?" Graham answered. Gordon was a big, cool fourth-grader back when we were puny first-graders. We had always hoped we would be as cool as him one day.

"What? Why would Gordon Armstrong walk into our class? He's in seventh grade," I said.

"I don't know, you just said, 'Guess who walked through the door?' so I thought I would guess Gordon Armstrong," Graham said, looking like that was a perfectly normal answer.

"Well, it wasn't Gordon. Let me give you a hint. She's someone you really like, and she can cut great heart shapes out of paper."

Graham's face went white, except for his lips. They were purple from his Popsicle.

"*Kelly?* Kelly came back to school?" Graham shouted. He started pacing around the room. "I can't believe it," he said. "This plan was perfect. I even got Popsicles and soda pop out of it. How could this happen?"

"I don't know—everything seemed to go bad. I was paired up with Heidi for about one minute. Then Kelly walked in and ruined that, and now I'm stuck with Lizzy."

"No way, you have to be Lizzy's partner? That's the worst," Graham said.

"Yeah, tell me about it," I said, dropping into a big chair. I had tried to follow manly rule number three, but it was no use. Graham plopped himself onto the couch. We both just sat there in silence thinking about our lousy luck and how terrible this dance was going to be. Finally, Graham spoke up.

"So who did Kelly get matched up with? Was it Brad?" he asked.

"No. It was Matt Lindenheimer. Brad is dancing with Suzy," I said.

"How did that happen? Brad is a lot taller than Matt," Graham said.

"That's what I thought, too. But Mrs. Gibson said it's just Brad's big hair that makes him look so tall."

"Hmm, so Kelly would rather dance with the smart kid, huh? She likes brains more than beauty," Graham said in a quiet voice, shaking his head.

"What are you talking about, Graham? She just got assigned to dance with Matt. It doesn't mean she likes him," I said.

"Sorry, I was just thinking out loud," Graham said. "Well, one way or another, I'm going to make this work. I don't know how, but mark my words: I *will* dance with Kelly."

"I hope you're right. I don't know how I'll ever be able to dance with Heidi. I would settle for just not having to dance with Lizzy," I said. I looked out the window. Graham's mom's car was pulling into the driveway. "Well, I'd better go, Graham.

Enjoy your soda pop and Popsicles. I hope you feel better."

"Hey, I'm not really sick," Graham said.

"Oh, yeah. I almost forgot." I walked out the door, passing Graham's mom.

I said hi and told her I just stopped by to see how he was doing. She thanked me for being a nice friend and pulled a cookie out of her grocery sack for my walk home.

I kicked a pinecone up the street. Little pieces broke off as it rolled. By the time I got home, the pinecone was almost gone.

My grandma and grandpa's big brown car was parked in our driveway. I hoped they weren't staying for dinner. I was not in the mood to have Grandpa picking things off my plate with his dirty fork.

"Hey, partner," Grandpa yelled as I walked into the house. He grabbed my hand and shook my arm all over the place like he was trying to pull it right off of my body.

"Hi, Gramps. Hi, Grandma," I said.

"Don't I get a hug from my favorite grandson?"

Grandma said. Not only was I getting a hug, but her wrinkly lips with bright red lipstick were all puckered up and heading toward me. I turned just in time to get the kiss on my cheek. It tickled a little. I know girls aren't supposed to shave, but sometimes I wonder if my grandma should shave off some of those whiskers on her face. They aren't thick like a man's beard, but they still tickle when she kisses you.

"So what have you been up to, partner? And why do you look so sad?" Gramps asked, putting his fists up like he wanted to box me or something.

"Nothing much, and I'm not really too sad. Although I did find out today that I have to dance with Lizzy at our class hoedown next month. I'm not too excited about that," I said.

"Oh, she can't be that bad. I'm sure you'll have a wonderful time," Grandma said. "Hoedowns are great fun."

"That's right," Gramps interrupted. "Your grandma and I used to square-dance every Saturday night back in the good old days. We were the best hoedown dancers around. Weren't we, honey?" Gramps said.

"Well, I don't know if we were the best, dear. But we did have a dandy time," Grandma answered.

"What do you mean, you don't know if we were the best? Of course we were the best! Everyone knew that," Grandpa said, hopping around and kicking his feet up in the air. "You've got dancing in your blood, Raymond," he added.

"You'd better stop that," Grandma called after Gramps. "You shouldn't be doing that with your bad hips." She chased him around the room trying to catch him.

"Well, I've never danced before, and I don't think I want to try with Lizzy," I said.

"You'll see, partner," Gramps said, "you'll love it." He kept hopping and dancing right out of the room and into the kitchen. I followed him in and sat down in my chair.

All of that dancing must have tired Gramps out, because he finally grabbed the chair right next to me and just kind of fell into it. He was breathing hard.

"Whew...Don't get old, partner," he said, patting me on my knee.

"I'll try not to," I replied. I was hoping he was just resting and would get up and sit somewhere else. But no such luck. He picked up the paper napkin in front of him, opened it, and stuck in his collar like a bib. This meant business.

I love Gramps and all. And it's not just that he takes food off of my plate. But whenever Gramps comes over, I get kinda sick watching him eat. Mom says I'm rude for feeling that way, but I can't help it. He shovels so much food in his mouth at a time. And he doesn't even finish what's in his mouth before he shoves more in there. There are always bits of chewed-up food falling out of his mouth when he opens it to put more in. It's disgusting! And even when I try not to watch him, I can still hear him. When he opens his mouth to load up, he makes this wheezing noise, like a broken vacuum. And then when he starts chewing, he makes this sick groaning noise with his voice.

Then a brilliant idea popped into my brain. Grandma sat down in a chair at the other end of the table. "Hey, Gramps, don't you want to sit by your lovely wife?"

"Nah, I sit by her every day. I'm taking a break," he said, laughing. He laughed until he started coughing. Mom patted him on the back. "And besides," he said, "this seat is closer to the bathroom, in case I need a quick getaway, if you know what I mean." He smiled at me and winked, like I knew what he meant. I didn't really know what he meant, but it didn't sound very good.

We were having pork chops, mashed potatoes, peas, and salad. As we passed the food around the table, there was nothing that Gramps didn't put on his plate. Even when there wasn't room for any more, he just piled it on top of his other food. I could tell this was going to be ugly.

Everyone dug in. In no time at all, the wheezing, sucking sound and the groaning began. My appetite was gone and I couldn't even eat a bite.

"Eat your food, Raymond," Dad said.

"I'm not that hungry. And I really don't like peas."

"Hey, partner," Gramps said. "Try your grandpa's old trick."

I looked over at his plate. He was smashing all of his peas into his mashed potatoes until it was a light green gooey mess. I felt queasy just looking at it and thought I might even puke. Then Gramps did something that put me over the edge. After taking a bite of his green potato-and-pea mixture, he pulled his fork out of his mouth. It still had some of the potato goo and a little piece of pork chop dangling from it. Then the fork headed toward my plate.

"I'll help you get rid of a few of these," Gramps said, sticking that nasty fork into my peas and scooping up a pile. He leaned over my plate and shoved the fork into his mouth so he wouldn't lose any peas. Unfortunately, one of the peas fell from either the fork or his mouth onto my potatoes. It was more than I could handle.

"Excuse me please!" I yelled, pushing my chair back and running into the bathroom. I stayed there for a long time. After a while, my mom knocked on the door.

"Raymond, are you all right in there?" she asked.

"Yeah, I'm fine," I said. "It's just that . . . well, Gramps . . ."

"I know, sweetie," she interrupted. "I saw him."

I opened the door and asked her if I had to finish my dinner.

"No, not tonight," she answered. "I'll make you up a new plate and put it in the refrigerator in case you want it later."

I went to my room. I hoped I didn't make Gramps feel bad, but I figured he was probably happy just finishing the rest of my dinner.

6

Closed for Cleaning

THE NEXT MORNING I woke up starving. Mom made heart-shaped pancakes and hot chocolate for breakfast to celebrate Valentine's Day. I ate tons of pancakes and drank four big cups of hot chocolate. So far things were going great. I finished breakfast, put my bag of valentines in my backpack, and ran out the door.

Graham came out of his house with a big smile on his face and a plastic grocery bag full of valentines.

"Why don't you carry them in your backpack?" I asked.

"I am carrying them in my backpack. These are just more valentines that didn't fit," Graham said, holding up his backpack to show me how full it was. "After you left the other day, I decided to make a few extra valentines for Kelly. I didn't sign them. I want to see if she can figure out it's me."

"How many extra did you make?"

"I don't know, about twenty," Graham said.

"Whoa, isn't that a little too much?" I asked.

"Listen, Raymond. Take it from your manly coach," Graham said. "You can never do too much for your girlfriend. You can't talk to her too much, wave at her too much, and there is no way on the planet you can give her too many valentines. Remember that. It's rule number four."

"Right," I said. "Thanks again for being my coach. I don't know what I would do without your help."

"Don't mention it, *hermano*. That's what friends— and manly coaches—are for."

We walked as fast as we could to get to school early. Our class Valentine's Day party would be in the afternoon, but Graham wanted to put the extra valentines he made for Kelly in her box without anyone seeing.

Luckily, we got there before the other kids. The

door was open, but Mrs. Gibson must have been in the office or somewhere else. All of the valentine boxes were on the back tables. "Okay, you stand by the door and watch for Kelly—I don't want her to see me. We need a code word or something. If she comes in, yell out, 'Underwear!'"

"Underwear?" I said.

"Yeah, underwear," Graham said. Then he headed back to the boxes. He looked around for a while and then called back. "Hey, which one is Kelly's? I don't see her name on any of these."

"It's in the middle with all of the really good hearts on it. You can't miss it," I said. "She wrote her name in hearts."

I looked down the hall to make sure Kelly wasn't coming. I didn't want to yell "Underwear!" if I could avoid it. A few people started coming through the door, but no sign of Kelly. Heidi and Diane came in talking.

"Happy Valentine's Day, Raymond," Heidi said, smiling.

"Happy Valentine's Day to you, too, Heidi," I said

back. I tried to follow manly rule number four and come up with something funny or clever to say to her, but I couldn't think of anything. As I stood there trying to be manly and talk to Heidi, I must have forgotten to look for Kelly, because all of a sudden I noticed Kelly was already in the classroom.

"*Underwear, underwear!*" I yelled. "*UNDER-WEAR!*"

Heidi, Diane, and everyone else in the class turned to see why I was screaming "Underwear." I just stood there with a blank look on my face, trying to pretend that nothing had happened. Everyone started laughing.

That wasn't funny or clever, I thought to myself. And definitely not manly. Just then Lizzy spotted Mrs. Gibson walking down the hall.

"Mrs. Gibson, Mrs. Gibson, Raymond just yelled 'Underwear' for no good reason," Lizzy tattled, running out to meet our teacher.

"Not now, Lizzy," Mrs. Gibson answered, passing her and entering our class. Lizzy stormed back into the room and gave me a mean glare.

"Okay, let's get started," Mrs. Gibson said. She was wearing a necklace made of big red, white, and pink hearts. "Is everyone having a happy Valentine's Day so far?"

"No," David blurted out.

Mrs. Gibson must have been in a good mood, because she didn't get mad at David. Instead she said, "Then we'll just have to make sure your day gets better, won't we?"

"I am!" Lizzy blurted out. "I'm having a great day. By the way, that necklace is very beautiful. It goes well with your . . . hair."

It goes well with gray hair? I thought to myself. Lizzy is such a weirdo.

"Thank you, Lizzy," Mrs. Gibson said. "I hope you all brought your valentines. We'll deliver them to the boxes this afternoon at our party. But first, we need to get through all of our work."

Suddenly, as Mrs. Gibson was talking, I realized drinking four cups of hot chocolate this morning might not have been a good idea. I had to go to the bathroom . . . and *bad*. I looked at the clock. We still had an hour and a half until recess. There was no way I could wait that long. I raised my hand.

"Yes, Raymond," Mrs. Gibson said.

"May I use the restroom?" I asked, squirming around in my chair.

"Fine, but hurry back."

I jumped up and ran out the door. "Walk, please," I heard Mrs. Gibson calling from the classroom. I slowed down to a fast walk. But as soon as I turned the corner I started to run again. I ran as fast as I could. When I tried to push the bathroom door open, I bounced back and fell to the floor.

Huh, how can this be locked? I thought. A little stand-up sign stood on the floor in front of the door. CLOSED FOR CLEANING, it said. I must have run right past it. I knocked on the door, but no one answered. I needed to get in there. There was no way I would make it down to the bathrooms at the other end of the school. The kindergarten class had bathrooms in it, but I wasn't going to burst into the kindergarten class to use their bathroom. I jumped around like crazy in the hall, waiting for the janitor to come back. If I couldn't get into the bathroom quick, I was going to have a serious accident.

After what seemed like forever, I had an idea. I couldn't believe I was even considering this, but it was the only thing left: the girls' bathroom. I had never set foot inside the girls' bathroom, and I'm sure if Graham were here he'd say, "Manly rule number five: Never go inside a girls' bathroom." But this was an emergency. I took one last look both ways down the hall and then burst through the door. It was pink instead of blue like the boys' bathroom. But that didn't matter at this point. I finished my business, washed my hands, and strolled back out the door.

"What are you doing, Raymond?" I heard a familiar voice say. It was Heidi. "Are you using the pink bathroom because it's Valentine's Day?" She laughed. "Isn't that going a little too far to celebrate a holiday?"

"No . . . I . . . I just went in there . . . I mean, I had to use the girls' because the boys' bathroom is closed for cleaning. See?" I said, pointing to the sign in front of the door. Only now the sign was gone. "Wait, it was here a minute ago," I said. I pushed on the door, which was open now, too.

"*Sure,*" she said. "Your secret's safe with me." Then she walked into the girls' bathroom, and I turned and went back to class. I thought about how this day was not turning out so manly. I mean, right in the middle of talking to her, I yell out "Underwear!" and then she sees me coming out of the girls' bathroom. I hoped my poem to her would make up for all of this unmanliness.

It seemed like the afternoon would never come. You could tell everyone was excited for our Valentine's Day party. Nobody could sit still.

Finally, it was time. "All right, students, while I am setting up for our party, why don't you get your valentines from your backpacks and deliver them to each box," Mrs. Gibson said.

Everyone jumped up and ran to their backpacks. For the next few minutes we all bunched around the boxes in the back of the room, stuffing valentines into the small slots cut into the tops of the decorated boxes. Mrs. Gibson even had a box on her desk. A huge valentine was next to her box that must have been too big to fit inside. I took a closer look to see who it was from. *Happy Valentine's Day to the best teacher in the world, from your favorite student, Lizzy,* it read on the front of the big heart.

After we finished our valentine deliveries, Lizzy's mom came in to help out. She'd brought a big box of cupcakes. Graham and I ran over to her to get the first ones. But just as we both reached for a cupcake, she pulled the box away.

"Not so fast," she said. "The first one goes to your wonderful teacher." She flipped her hair around, walked over, and handed Mrs. Gibson the cupcake. I couldn't believe it. She was a teacher's pet just like Lizzy. She even had that same crinkled-up look on her face. Graham and I grabbed the next two cupcakes and went back to check on our boxes.

"Okay, kids," Mrs. Gibson said when the bell rang, "have a wonderful Valentine's Day. Please do not open your valentines in the school ... wait until you get home." We all raced to the back and grabbed our boxes. Mine felt really heavy.

Graham and I went to his house to open our valentines together. We sat down in the middle of his room. "Okay, Raymond," Graham started, "the only rule is that you can't keep anything a secret. If you get something interesting from anyone, you have to tell."

"That works for me," I said. I never get anything interesting anyway. Neither does Graham, for that matter. But for some reason, he thought this year was going to be different.

"Okay, here's my first one," I said, opening the first valentine I pulled out of my box. *"Have a Happy Valentines or I'll punch you, From ? ... P.S. I'm going to punch you tomorrow anyway."* I could tell from the handwriting and from the punching that it was from David.

"Well, that one wasn't so good," I said, reaching for another.

"How about this?" Graham said. "It's from Eden. It just says, *To Graham, From Eden.*"

"That's pretty boring," I said.

"But wait, look what it says on the candy hearts in the envelope," he said, dumping three colored candies into his hand. "This one says *Be Mine* and this pink one says *Your Girl* and, whoa—this one says *Hot Stuff!* Do you think Eden likes me? I mean, she obviously thinks I'm hot stuff."

"Are you serious? Those hearts all say stuff like that. I never read them, I just grab a few and drop them in the envelope."

"Not me," Graham said. "I read each one and carefully choose which goes in each valentine. I'll bet everyone does that except you." He looked at me like I was a moron.

"Wow, listen to this," I said. "This one says I'm cute!"

"What? Who's it from?" Graham yelled. He looked a little mad that I got that one instead of him.

"I don't know, it just says, *From ?*" I said, trying to examine the handwriting. It didn't look like Heidi's. Actually, the handwriting was really bad. "Maybe whoever it was tried to disguise their writing so I wouldn't be able to figure out who they were."

Graham dug through his box faster and faster. "I've got to find Kelly's," he said, ripping open envelopes.

"Oh my gosh!" I said. "Here's another one. It says my eyes are beautiful. Wow, I never thought I had beautiful eyes, but I guess someone thinks I do." This was turning out to be the best Valentine's Day ever. I tore open another, wondering if I had more secret admirers.

"Whoa, this one stinks like perfume or something," I said, waving my hand in front of my nose.

"Give me that, Raymond," Graham said, grabbing the valentine from me. "What did you say that last one said?"

"You mean the one that says I have beautiful eyes?"

"Yeah, that one. Let me see it."

"It's in that pile," I said, pointing to the pile of papers and valentines. I opened another one while he sorted through my opened valentines.

"No way," I said. "Here's another: *Your lips are so*

shapely. I have shapely lips? What does that mean?"

"Okay, give me that one, too," Graham yelled, grabbing the valentine. "I thought you said Kelly's valentine box was the one with the perfect hearts on it!" He grabbed my box. "Look at your box, Raymond: ten perfect hearts. *Ten!*"

"So what? What are you saying?" I said, pulling my box out of his hands.

"I'm saying I put all the extra valentines I made for Kelly in your box!" he shouted, looking sad and angry.

"Oh, no!" I said. "I forgot Kelly gave me a handful of hearts for my box. The hearts I cut out looked like eggs, so she gave me her extras. But didn't you see her name on her box? I told you it was spelled out in little hearts."

"No, I just saw this big *K* on the front and thought it stood for *Kelly*," Graham said.

"That's an *R* for *Raymond*," I said. I copied her idea. Although, as I looked at it again, it did kind of look like a *K*.

"Well, that's just great!" Graham said, waving

a handful of valentines in the air. "Now Kelly isn't going to have *any* valentines from me! She'll think I don't like her at all."

"So does this mean my lips aren't shapely?" I said, trying to make Graham laugh. But I couldn't even get a grin out of him.

"Come on," I said. "We can fix it. Let's gather up all of these valentines you wrote to Kelly and bring them to her house. We'll ring the doorbell and run. . . . It'll be fun."

Graham's face broke out into a smile. "Great idea! It's more personal that way." He picked up the valentines and we headed for the front door.

"Hey, Mom, I'm going outside with Raymond," he yelled.

"Be back before dinner," she called back from somewhere in the house.

Kelly's house was about three blocks away. When we got there, we looked around and made our plan.

"Okay," Graham said, "you set the valentines in front of the door. After I ring the doorbell, we'll run over there behind those bushes by the street. From there we can see her open the door."

We crept up to the door. I set the valentines down while Graham rang the bell. I was setting them up in a nice, neat pile when all of a sudden I heard the bell ring. I tried to stand up, but Graham ran right over me and tripped. He fell on top of me and we both struggled to get up. I pushed Graham off of me, made it to my feet, and ran like crazy. Unfortunately, before Graham could get up, the door opened. I could see it was Kelly. Graham finally jumped up and started running.

"Hi, Graham," Kelly said.

Graham didn't answer and just kept running. I watched Kelly pick up the valentines and close the door. We waited for a couple of minutes, then began walking home.

"Man, Raymond, what were you doing in my way? Why didn't you move when I rang the bell?" Graham asked in a frustrated voice.

"It was kind of hard to move with you *sitting on me*!" I answered.

"Well . . . I was . . . um . . ." I could tell Graham was trying to say something but didn't know what it was. "Okay, I guess I was sitting on you." We both started laughing.

"At least she'll know who gave her the valentines," I said, patting Graham on his shoulder. We walked home feeling pretty good about the day.

7

Gray Hair
and Glasses

THE NEXT DAY at school, everyone was talking about their valentines. Heidi came up to me and said, "I think you're pretty tidy, too, Raymond." It sounded funny being called tidy. I wondered if Heidi thought my poem to her was a little weird.

"Sorry," I said. "*Tidy* was the only word I could think of that rhymed with *Heidi*." She just laughed and sat down at her desk. I went to my desk as well. Just as I sat down, Kelly walked up to me.

"Hey, Raymond," she said. "Why did Graham give me this valentine at my house yesterday? I mean, the others he gave me were so nice." She dropped a valentine on my desk and stood there waiting.

I picked it up and read it out loud. "'Have a happy Valentine's Day or I'll punch you . . . P.S. I'm going to punch you tomorrow anyway.'"

Just then David walked by. "Thanks for re-minding me," he said. "I almost forgot." He slugged me in the arm and walked away. I felt a tear start to form in my eye, but I stayed strong. *Be manly, be manly,* I repeated in my mind. There was no way I was going to break manly rule num-ber one ever again.

"Sorry, Kelly, that valentine was to me from David," I said, rubbing my arm. "I don't know how it got mixed up with the rest of Graham's valentines to you."

"Thanks, Raymond, it didn't sound like Graham," she said. She turned and went to her desk. I decided I wouldn't tell Graham about that little mix-up. Just then I heard my name being called.

"Raymond and Graham, could you both come here, please?" Mrs. Gibson called out. We hurried over to her. She was in the back of the class sitting at a table.

"Have a seat," she said, pointing to two chairs she had set up especially for us. I couldn't tell if she was angry or happy. I think it was her wrinkles that always confused me, because sometimes when she laughed, the wrinkles around her eyes and mouth made her look really mad.

"I have already had several students speak to me this morning, and even one parent called concerning the valentines you two gave out," she said. "They claim you wrote mean poems that hurt their feelings. For instance, Mrs. Shaw called wondering why Graham wrote a poem about Brad's big hair."

Now I could tell for sure that Mrs. Gibson was not happy. "I know you two, and I'm sure you probably didn't mean to hurt anyone's feelings, but I can see why some of the kids are upset. For instance," she said, picking up a card from her desk, "Here is the valentine you wrote to me, Raymond.

"Your glasses are huge and your hair is gray.
I hope you have a happy Valentine's Day."

I looked at her big glasses and gray hair as she read my card out loud. I had to admit it was a pretty good poem. It was a great description of her. However, as she raised her eyes from the card, she didn't seem to see the beauty of the poem.

"Can you see why these things you wrote, while they rhyme and may be true, might hurt someone's feelings?" she said, adjusting her huge glasses on her nose. She looked a little sad.

Suddenly, I understood what she meant. Maybe a good rhyme doesn't automatically make a good valentine. I looked into Mrs. Gibson's eyes and, for a moment, instead of a teacher, I saw an old lady who maybe didn't want to be reminded that she was old and gray. Maybe she would rather have had a valentine that just said, *Thanks for being a good teacher, Happy Valentine's Day*. I looked over at Brad Shaw and thought that maybe he can't help having huge hair. Obviously, it just grows like that. Maybe he didn't want to be reminded of it in a valentine. I felt terrible. I looked over at Graham and could tell he felt bad, too.

"We're sorry," we both said at the same time.

"We didn't mean to hurt anyone's feelings," I said. "We just thought we were making good poems."

"I know," Mrs. Gibson said. "And the truth is, they were pretty clever. But always try to think about how the person who receives your poem will feel." She sat back and looked at us for a minute. Then she smiled and said, "That's all, you two." We both stood up and went to our seats.

At recess, Graham talked to Brad and told him he was sorry about the poem. "I really think your hair is cool," he said. "It makes you look like you're three inches taller."

Then we went around and apologized to everyone else who got one of our poems. Well, everyone but Lizzy.

That afternoon we had our first dance practice for the spring hoedown. We all walked in a line down to the lunchroom.

"Okay, everyone, please line up next to your dance partners," Mrs. Gibson said. Slowly, I made my way into the line next to Lizzy.

"By the way, Raymond," Lizzy said, sticking her snooty face up close to mine, "*crinklier* and *stinklier* aren't even words." Then she flipped her bouncy curls away from me.

"Sorry, Lizzy," I said. "I didn't mean to make you—"

"I don't care," Lizzy interrupted. "I told on you anyway."

Oh, well, I thought to myself, *her face does look all crinklier.*

Graham raised his hand. "Mrs. Gibson," he said. "I don't have a partner."

"Oh, that's right," Mrs. Gibson said. "We have one extra boy." She paused a moment to think. "Okay, this is what we'll do. Since we have one extra boy, could I get a volunteer to—"

My hand shot up in an instant. I knew what she was going to say, and I was going to be the first to volunteer. She was about to ask for a volunteer to sit out. You know, not to be in the dance. I jumped up and down with my hand in the air.

"Raymond, you didn't let me finish," she said.

"I know, but whatever it is, I'll do it," I said.

"Great, that's very nice of you, Raymond. It will help us all out," she said. "Why don't you come over here by my side."

Lizzy gave me a nasty look. I gave her one back and proudly walked up next to Mrs. Gibson.

"Okay, boys. Everyone move up one spot to fill in Raymond's place. And Graham, you go to the end next to Suzy."

"But don't you think I would fit in better right here?" he said, pointing to Matt, who was next to Kelly.

"No, the end by Suzy will be just fine," she said. Graham moped over to the end of the boys next to Suzy.

"Okay, since we have one extra boy, Raymond has volunteered to be my partner," Mrs. Gibson said. "Raymond and I will be teaching you the dance up here in front."

WHAT?! I screamed inside my head. *Dance with the teacher?* I didn't know what was worse, dancing with Lizzy or dancing with Mrs. Gibson. Even though Lizzy and I were enemies, at least she was a kid. I looked around at the crowd. Everyone was laughing and pointing at me. Even Graham was busting up. David looked like he was going to fall over. I glanced up at Mrs. Gibson, who was staring down at me with a big smile.

"Thanks for volunteering, Raymond," she said. I could tell she sensed my embarrassment, but somehow I think she enjoyed it. I knew I couldn't hurt her feelings again after my valentine poem, so I just looked up and smiled back.

Finally, everyone calmed down, and for most of the next hour, Mrs. Gibson taught us the dance. There was a lot of bowing to each other, skipping, and hooking arms and going in circles. Mrs. Gibson's bony arms were pretty strong. Whenever we had to hook arms and swing around in a circle, she would almost pull me right off my feet.

"Okay, I think we are ready to try it with the

music," Mrs. Gibson said. She walked over and pushed the button on the stereo and hurried back to her spot next to me in front of the class.

It was square-dancing music. You know, the kind with the fiddles playing and some guy telling you when to do-si-do and stuff.

"Okay, everyone, in your places and get ready. Watch me and Raymond to see when to start," Mrs. Gibson said, bending her knees with the rhythm.

"Ready . . . and . . . begin!" she yelled out.

Dancing with the music was hard. It was going so much faster than we had practiced. Mrs. Gibson was basically dragging me around to keep up with the music.

I looked at everyone else. They all seemed to be lost. Some people were bowing when they should have been going in a circle, while others were skipping around each other do-si-doing. After about a minute of out-of-control dancing, Mrs. Gibson turned off the music.

"Okay, now that we have all heard how fast it

is," she said, "let's try it from the beginning. And remember, watch up here and follow us." She pushed the button and hurried back.

The music started again and all of a sudden, without even my thinking about it, my legs were bouncing up and down to the rhythm. When the guy in the song started talking, I suddenly knew what I was doing. And not only did I know what I was doing, I was liking it. I looked around at everyone else. Some were getting it better than others, but no one was dancing as well as I was.

I couldn't believe what was going on. I was skipping perfectly to the beat and I do-si-doed at exactly the right time. When the song ended, I actually felt a little sad, like I wanted it to go on longer.

A bunch of people came up to me and teased me about having to dance with Mrs. Gibson. David slugged me and said, "What's wrong, too scared to dance with a girl? Baby Raymond has to dance with the teacher?"

"I'm not a baby!" I yelled. David just laughed

and walked away. But maybe he was right. Did I look like a baby, having to dance with the teacher? I started going through the manly rules in my head when I felt a slap on my back.

"I really owe you one, *hermano*," Graham said, putting his hand on my shoulder.

"What are you talking about?" I said.

"Are you serious?" Graham answered. "If you hadn't volunteered to dance with Mrs. Gibson, it would have been me."

"Whoa, I didn't think of that," I said. "You really do owe me one. I can't believe it. I thought for sure she was going to ask for a volunteer to sit out and not have to dance."

"Yeah, bummer," Graham said. "But at least you're not dancing with Lizzy."

"I guess . . . although I'm still not sure what's worse," I said. "You know Lizzy got mad at me about her valentine poem. She said *crinklier* and *stinklier* aren't real words. Even though she's a girl, she obviously doesn't understand poetic words like we do. And anyway, I actually think *crinklier* is a word."

"Sure it is," Graham agreed. "Like my shirt is much crinklier than your shirt."

"Right," I said. As we walked back to the classroom, we compared things that were crinklier than other things. We both agreed that nothing was crinklier than Lizzy's face.

Being Mature

THE NEXT MONDAY at school, Mrs. Gibson passed out cards to each of us.

"Please take these invitations home and show them to your parents," Mrs. Gibson said. "The maturation program is coming up this Friday for you and your parents."

I had heard about the maturation program and about how embarrassing it is. I did not want to go. Graham, on the other hand, couldn't wait.

That afternoon our class was in the library checking out books. Graham and I were in the back corner looking for a book about sports.

"This is going to be great!" he said in his loudest whisper. "You know, the maturation program."

"I don't want to go at all," I said. "It will be so embarrassing."

"Are you kidding? It will be great! I can't wait to mature. We'll get to shave, we'll have deep voices, and all that good stuff. It means we'll be that much closer to being men. Plus, if you really don't want to feel like a baby, don't you think it's a good idea to find out as much as you can about how to be mature?"

I thought about that for a minute. "Maybe you're right. Being mature is the exact opposite of being a baby."

"Of course I'm right. After all, I am your coach," Graham said. "Which brings me to rule number five: Attend your maturation program and learn as much as possible about being manly."

"Yeah, although I still wish I didn't have to hear about all of that stuff sitting next to my dad," I said.

"Not me. I want to find out exactly when I'm

going to start shaving and being mature," Graham said.

"How are they going to know?" I said. "They can't tell you when."

"Well, they definitely know more than I know," Graham said.

Later that day, after school, Diane invited me and Graham to come over to her house to jump on her trampoline with her and Heidi. Graham told me this would be a great time to practice my manly skills of talking to Heidi more. "Don't worry, I'll help you get started," he promised.

When we got to Diane's house, I called my mom and told her where I was. Then I ran back outside, where Graham and the girls were already jumping.

"So, Heidi," Graham said, "Raymond wants to talk to you about something." He looked at me as if to say, *Go ahead, that was your cue.* Everyone stopped jumping and stared at me.

"I do?" I asked, turning to Graham. He slapped his forehead with the palm of his hand.

"Yes, you do. . . . Remember?" he said, trying to get me started, but I couldn't think of anything to say. I stood there straining my brain trying to think of something.

"Well, it must have been really important," Heidi said, starting to jump around again. Graham gave up on me and started his own conversation.

"Is everyone as excited as me about becoming mature on Friday?" Graham asked proudly.

"Yeah, I'm sure you're going to walk into the maturation program a scrawny little kid and leave an hour later a man." Heidi laughed as she bounced over Graham, who was lying down in the middle of the trampoline. I was sitting on the side by the springs, taking my shoes off.

"Right," Diane said, following Heidi and jumping over Graham. "You're going to need a lot more than a maturation program to become a man."

"Oh, yeah? Well, I'm more mature than you guys," Graham said.

"You? You're only about half as tall as me," Diane said, looking down at Graham.

"But I'm twice as tough," Graham answered back, standing up.

"Oh, yeah? Prove it," Diane said, pushing him in the chest. They both started jumping around trying to knock each other down. After being thrown down five times in a row, Graham just lay there and yelled, "You win! I give up!"

Heidi jumped up and grabbed Diane's hand and lifted it high in the air. "And the new mature champion of the fourth grade is . . . Diane Dunstin!"

We all cheered and laughed, even Graham. Diane took a bow. Then we got up and all started jumping together. At four thirty, I had to leave. Graham left with me. As we walked down the sidewalk, I turned to him and said, "Diane really got you good. Maybe *she* should be my manly coach instead of you."

Graham looked at me. I tried to keep a straight face, but I started to laugh. Graham just shook his head. "I could have taken her down if I'd wanted."

"Right. See you tomorrow, *hermano*," I said as we got to Graham's driveway.

Late Bloomers

WHEN I GOT to my house, I showed my mom the maturation-program invitation.

"Oh, how wonderful, my baby is growing up." There it was again. *Baby*.

"Mom, do you really think I'm a baby?" I asked.

"You'll always be my baby," she answered, pulling me close and giving me a hug. That wasn't what I'd wanted to hear.

"No, that's not what I mean," I said. My mom looked down at me.

"What's the matter? Aren't you excited about your maturation program?"

"No. I don't really want to go," I said.

"Of course you do, sweetie," she said. "I went with your sister, and it will be nice to go with your father. After all, you will be maturing soon."

"Mom! Don't say that!" I yelled.

"Well, it's true," she said. "It's just part of growing up. Don't you want to mature?"

"Yes, I want to mature. I don't want to be called a *baby* anymore. It's just that I don't want to discuss my maturing with my mom," I said.

"Oh, for heaven's sake, don't be silly," she said.

That night at dinner, my mom had to bring it up again. "Honey," she said to Dad, "can you take off work a little early on Friday? Raymond has his maturation program at school."

From the look on Dad's face, he was more nervous than I was. "Oooh, I, uh . . . aren't they a little young for this? Or isn't this something you would like to go to, dear?" Dad said.

"No, I think this would be a nice father-and-son activity," Mom answered.

"What's the big deal?" Geri snorted. "They're just going to tell you that you're a little dork now and soon you'll be a *big* dork." Mom gave her a dirty look.

"I'll be there, pal," Dad said to me, smiling, though he still looked a little nervous. My dad's a great guy. He loves to play catch with me, take me fishing, and all that fun stuff. But when it comes to having to talk about serious things, he'd rather leave that to my mom.

The week flew by, and in no time at all it was Friday. All day, Graham was excited about the maturation program and couldn't wait for it to start. Deep down, I think he still thought that going to the meeting would make him more mature. We ended our dance practice early so we would be finished in time for the program.

We left the lunchroom where we practiced and walked quietly back to our classroom. I could smell old-lady perfume on my arm where Mrs. Gibson and I had to swing around.

Within a few minutes, parents started to arrive for the program. As they showed up, Mrs. Gibson had them stand in the back of the class until it was time to start. The girls were having their program in the library, and we were having ours in the auditorium. Within a few minutes, almost every parent was there, except mine. It was almost time to go, and my dad still hadn't arrived.

"Okay, girls," Mrs. Gibson said. "Why don't you show your mothers down to the library?" They all stood up and filed out of the room.

I looked out the door and down the hall, but there was still no sign of my dad. This would actually be perfect if he didn't show up. I could still learn all the stuff about being mature, but I wouldn't have to sit next to my dad and be embarrassed.

"Okay, boys," Mrs. Gibson said. "Your turn. You can show your fathers, or whoever came with you, to the auditorium." We all got up and headed down the hall. I followed the pack and sat in the back row. Graham was pulling his dad up to the front so he wouldn't miss anything. Graham's dad was also short. He was bald on top with a thick ring of red hair around the sides of his head.

A lady in a white nurse uniform walked onto the stage. "Hello, I want to welcome everyone to the maturation program," she said. "My name is

Nurse Suzanne. I work for the school district. And today—"

"Excuse me," interrupted a loud voice from the doorway. "Raymond, are you in here?"

I know that voice, I thought to myself. It was Gramps! I couldn't believe it. I stood up and waved to him.

"Sorry I'm late, everyone," Gramps said, even louder than before. "Have I missed anything?"

"You're just in time," Nurse Suzanne said. "We're about to begin."

"Wonderful," Gramps said, making his way to an empty seat next to me. "Raymond's dad is stuck in a meeting, so his mother called me. She thought Raymond would feel more comfortable with a man—even an old man." Gramps laughed. "Although I see you are a woman and you're teaching the class, so maybe it would be fine if Raymond's mother—"

"Gramps, just sit down," I interrupted, pulling his arm. He stopped talking and sat down next to me.

"Howdy, partner," Gramps said to me in his whisper voice, which was just about as loud as his regular voice. Nurse Suzanne started talking about how we need to wash our hair every day and use soap whenever we shower. She also told us we were probably going to get some pimples sometime soon. She talked about a bunch of other embarrassing stuff, and finally it was almost over.

"Are there any questions?" she asked the audience.

"I have one," Graham said, raising his hand. "When do you think I'm going to get taller and be able to grow a mustache?"

I couldn't believe he was asking that. I felt embarrassed for Graham. However, not as embarrassed as I was about to feel for myself.

"Can I answer that?" my grandpa yelled out.

"Be my guest, sir," Nurse Suzanne answered.

"Great," Gramps said. "Now, where is the young man who asked that question?"

Graham stood up and waved at Gramps.

"Oh, you're Raymond's little friend," Gramps

started. "I thought you looked familiar. Well, let me tell you, both you and Raymond are still pretty small, and while the time will come someday for both of you to grow, judging from the size of you, it may not be for a long time. For instance, I was quite the late bloomer myself. I don't think I had to shave until I was in the army. And I don't know about you, but if Raymond here takes after his grandpa, he can count on being a late bloomer, too."

I couldn't believe this. Everyone in the whole auditorium was staring at us like we were crazy. David was laughing and pointing at me. His dad was also laughing. I started feeling dizzy. "I've got to go to the bathroom, Grandpa, I'll be right back," I said.

"Hey, not a bad idea," Gramps said. "I'll join you."

We got up and made our way out of the auditorium. I was so embarrassed I thought I was going to die.

"Well, I'm glad I could be here for you, partner," Gramps said, putting his arm around my shoulder. "I wouldn't want you to have to sit through this alone."

"Yeah, well . . . thanks, Gramps," I said. By the time we made it back, the meeting was over and everyone was leaving. There was a big box by the door with a sign on it that said TAKE ONE. It was full of bags that had little bottles of shampoo and sticks of deodorant in them.

"Hey, do I get one of those?" Gramps asked Nurse Suzanne, who was standing by the door.

"Sure, help yourself," she said with a smile.

We both grabbed a bag and left. Grandpa took me to get an ice-cream cone on the way home.

"One scoop for my grandson who just graduated from the maturation program," Gramps proudly told the girl at the ice-cream counter.

"Congratulations," she said, holding back her laughter. "What flavor would you like?"

"Chocolate," I said.

"Very mature choice, partner," Gramps said. "I'll take the same."

We ate our ice cream and Gramps dropped me off at home. I walked in, went straight to my room, and plopped onto my bed. What a lousy day.

10
Toilets and Toothbrushes

I LAY ON my bed for a while, not feeling any more mature than I had before the maturation program. There had to be more to not being a baby than shampoo and pimples. I thought about it for a few minutes. I got up and walked to the bathroom to wash my hands. They were sticky from the ice cream.

As I walked into the bathroom, something familiar caught my eye. I rushed up to the sink. There was my old Peter Penguin toothbrush. I couldn't believe it.

Peter Penguin was my favorite cartoon when

I was in kindergarten. I had Peter Penguin toys, shoes, clothes . . . everything. I even had Peter Penguin underwear. But by the time I was in the first grade, I had grown out of my Peter Penguin clothes and all of my friends stopped playing with Peter Penguin stuff.

I did, however, keep my Peter Penguin toothbrush. I thought no one could take that away from me. It was my all-time favorite. I don't even remember what I brushed my teeth with before I had that. Anyway, one day my toothbrush disappeared and a new plain blue one showed up in its place. Mom said she had replaced it because it was worn out and too small.

Anyway, when I walked into the bathroom and saw my old friend Peter Penguin on the counter by the sink, it felt like a miracle. How else could my favorite toothbrush simply appear in the bathroom? I picked it up. It did look pretty worn out, but I didn't care.

As I was examining my long-lost toothbrush, a terrible thought came over me. If Graham were here, I'll bet he would say, "Rule number six: No cartoon character toothbrushes." Maybe I was a baby after all. I mean, I cry when I get hurt, I'm embarrassed about the maturation program, and now I want to brush my teeth with a Peter Penguin toothbrush. *Why does being manly have to be so hard? I thought to myself.*

I walked over to the small garbage can next to the toilet and was about to throw it away. Then I thought to myself, *Maybe just one more brushing for old time's sake.*

Immediately, I rushed back to the sink and turned on the water. I usually don't brush my teeth during the day, but this was a special occasion. My old friend Peter Penguin and I were reunited at last. I put a little water and a dab of toothpaste on the brush, and in no time at all, I was scrubbing like crazy. I looked in the mirror and it seemed like my reflection was six years old again. Memories of good times passed through my mind. After spitting and rinsing my toothbrush, I stuck my mouth under the faucet and got a drink. I looked in the mirror again and smiled. My teeth looked whiter already. Yes, there was something magical about that toothbrush. I decided to keep it. Who cares if there is a rule about cartoon character toothbrushes? I was never going to tell Graham anyway.

I ran out of the bathroom and into the kitchen. Mom was on the phone with Grandma. "Hey, Mom, I found my toothbrush! I thought you threw it out, but it—"

"I'm on the phone, sweetie," she said. "Give me a couple of minutes."

I knew just the thing to do in those couple of minutes: brush my teeth again. I ran back to the bathroom, loaded up Peter with toothpaste, and started scrubbing. A few minutes later, I heard my mom.

"Raymond, I'm off the phone. What did you need?" she asked.

"Nothing, Mom," I said happily. "I was just wondering where you found my favorite Peter Penguin toothbrush. My teeth feel better than ever!"

"I'm sorry, Raymond, what toothbrush are you talking about?" she asked, walking into the bathroom.

"This one," I said, holding it up.

"Oh, dear!" Mom yelled, grabbing it from my hand. "Don't put that in your mouth! It's been in my cleaning bucket for ages. I use it to scrub corners and around the toilet."

All of a sudden it seemed like she was speaking in slow motion. I tried to talk but couldn't. "This was in the toilet?" I was finally able to say, feeling sick. The fresh, clean taste in my mouth suddenly disappeared, and terrible thoughts of what I had been scrubbing onto my teeth filled my brain.

"Yes, Raymond. I use that to clean the hard-to-reach areas of the toilet," she said.

"Aaaaah, yuck!" I yelled, spitting into the sink. Then I stuck my mouth under the faucet for about five minutes. *I'm going to die!* I thought as water from the faucet filled my mouth.

"Mom, how could you?" I yelled, turning off the water. "Why didn't you say anything about using

my toothbrush to clean toilets? And why did you leave it here on the counter for me to use?" I went back to spitting into the sink.

"I'm sorry, Raymond," she said, rubbing my back. "I was cleaning in here today and must have forgotten to put it away. I'm sure you'll be fine."

"You're sure I'll be fine?" I cried. "How can I be fine? I've been scrubbing my teeth with a toilet brush!"

I went to my room to lie down.

"Why don't you rest, and I'll bring you a snack," Mom said.

As I lay there wondering what was going to happen to me, Mom came back with a little plate of cookies.

"Mom, if I die from this, please don't tell anyone that it was from some toilet disease. That would be way too embarrassing. Just tell everyone I died trying to rescue you or something."

"Raymond, don't be silly. You're going to be fine," she said. "Have a cookie and a little rest."

I was still in my room when Dad came home.

Mom must have told him what happened. He opened my door and poked his head in. "Hey, bud, I hear you were chewing on the toilet plunger."

"Something like that," I said. "Do you think I'm going to die?"

"Nah, look at old Maggie. She drinks out of the toilet every day and she's fine," Dad said.

I thought about that for a while, and he was right. Maybe I would survive after all.

That night, my dumb plain blue toothbrush had never looked better.

11

Dr. Fat Fingers Strikes Again

THE WEEKEND WENT by way too fast, and it was Monday all over again and we were walking to school. I ended up telling Graham all about my toothbrush experience. I thought he would bring up the fact that real men don't have cartoon character toothbrushes. But he didn't.

"Well, speaking of teeth," he said, looking down at the ground. "I'm getting out of school early today."

"No way," I said. "Where are you going?"

"I have to go to Dr. Fat Fingers for a checkup," he said sadly.

"Are you serious?" I replied. "All I can say is I'm sorry, *hermano*. I wouldn't wish a trip to Dr. Fat Fingers on my worst enemy. Not even on Lizzy."

Dr. Fat Fingers is the nickname we gave to Diane's dad, Dr. Dunstin. Almost all of my friends go to him for their dentist. He's a nice man, but he should definitely not be a dentist. Mom says he's a fine dentist and that we need to support our friends. But she never goes to him, just us kids.

Dr. Dunstin is a huge man. Diane told us he played basketball in college. He's at least a foot taller than my dad. Being tall isn't the problem . . . it's his fingers. They're *humongous*! They are at least twice as fat as a normal adult's fingers. They're probably great for playing basketball, but they are the absolute worst for working on kids' teeth. I mean, even though he can barely fit one of those fingers in your mouth, he insists on sticking at least two or three in at a time, whether they fit or not. It should be a rule that people with fingers that big should only be allowed to work on people with huge mouths. I felt sorry for Graham, but I was glad it was him and not me going to the dentist that day.

Dance practice went well, even without Graham. I have to admit that I was a little jealous that Zach was dancing with Heidi. During a break, I tried to follow manly rule number four and talk to Heidi as much as possible.

"Hi, Heidi. Are you having fun?" I asked.

"Yeah, sure. Are you?" she asked. "And where's Graham? Is he faking sick to get out of dancing today?"

"No, believe me, he'd much rather be here. He has a dentist appointment with Dr. Fat F—"

"Don't even say it!" interrupted Diane, who was listening.

"No, what I meant to say was . . . um . . ." I stood there, trying to think of something, when Mrs. Gibson started the music and we all ran back to our places.

After school, I called Graham to see how his visit to Dr. Fat Fingers went. His whole mouth was numb, so I couldn't understand him very well over the phone. He sounded funny, so I thought I would go down to his house to see if he looked funny, too.

Whenever I ride my bike to Graham's house, I always do the same thing. As soon as I get to his driveway, I jump off the back and let my bike ride by itself until it crashes on his lawn. Today was no different. But this time I was going a little too fast, and when I jumped off and let my bike go, it kept going longer than usual and crashed into the bushes. As I was dragging it out, Graham opened the door. He said something to me, but I couldn't understand. It sounded like he had a huge wad of gum in his mouth.

"What?" I said. "What are you saying?" Then I looked closer at him. "Whoa! Look at that bruise! I thought my last bruise was bad. But it was nothing compared to what Fat Fingers did to you!"

Graham looked at me like he was about to cry.

"Sorry, Graham." Then I thought about Graham's manly rule number one. "Hey, I thought rule number one was that real men never cry." Then I looked closer at his face. "Hey, you're not crying,"

I said. "You're laughing!" His face was still so numb his lips couldn't make a smiling shape. It was crazy. His lips and cheeks were all saggy. He looked like an old man, but without wrinkles.

"Wash thish," he said in a slurred voice, pinching himself on the cheek. "Doeshn't hurt."

"Whoa, that's great!" I said. "Can I try?" I picked up a stick from the ground and poked him in the cheek.

"Noshing," he said. Then he grabbed a bigger stick and smacked himself in the face.

"Nothing?" I asked.

"Noshing at all," Graham replied, with that same crazy smile and slurred voice.

"Hey, try this," I said, picking up a rock. "Press this on your face. Let's see if it will make a design." I pressed it hard against his cheek for about twenty seconds. "It worked!" I yelled. "Go look in the mirror."

After looking in the mirror, we searched for other things to press into his face. We tried a quarter, a bottle cap, a plastic army man, and the bottom of a

boot. While he was pressing the boot on his cheek, his eyes got all watery. He dropped the boot, walked into the bathroom, and closed the door.

"*YEEEEOOWWW!!!*" he yelled. I could hear him jumping around in the bathroom.

"Graham, are you all right?" I called to him.

Slowly, he opened the door. He had all sorts of imprints and cuts on his face. The numbness must have been wearing off, because he was holding his face in pain. I could definitely tell that he was *not* smiling anymore.

This really did end up being the day that Graham broke manly rule number one. But I wasn't going to call him a baby. I gave him a pat on the shoulder and told him he had better get some rest. Then I walked out the door, picked up my bike, and rode home.

12

Howdy, Pardner

FOR THE NEXT two weeks, we practiced every single day for our big hoedown. On Thursday, the day before our performance, Mrs. Gibson reminded us to wear Western clothes. She told us to look for bandanas to tie around our necks, and if any of us had cowboy boots, we could wear them also. Brad Shaw was the only person I knew who wore cowboy boots.

After school, Graham and I played basketball all afternoon. As we played, we talked about the dance. Graham still had hopes that somehow he would end up dancing with Kelly. I didn't say anything, but I knew that wasn't going to happen.

We kept playing until Graham had to go in and eat dinner. I picked up my backpack and ran home to do the same. When I got there, on my bed was a great red bandana, a new Western shirt, and, best of all, a real cowboy hat. I put on the hat and ran into the kitchen, where my mom was making one of my favorite dinners . . . spaghetti and meatballs.

"All right!" I said. "I love spaghetti! Hey, and thanks for all the cowboy stuff. It's great!"

"I just wanted you to be the most handsome cowboy out there tomorrow," Mom said, smiling.

"Well, I am kind of excited about it. Except for one thing . . . dancing with Mrs. Gibson," I said. "I just can't believe I have to dance with the teacher."

"Oh, it won't be so bad," Mom said.

After dinner I finished my homework and went to bed early. I closed my eyes for what seemed like a few seconds and it was morning. I had some cereal, brushed my teeth with my blue toothbrush, and headed down the street.

"Howdy, pardner. Nice shirt," I said to Graham, who was also in a Western shirt.

"You, too, cowboy," Graham answered. We both spoke with a Western accent.

"You reckon there's any chance of me dancin' with little ol' Kelly?" Graham said, walking bow-legged.

"Well, I reckon not, cowboy," I said. "It would take a heap of good luck for that to happen. How about me dancing with Heidi? Do you reckon that could still happen?"

"No, there ain't no way that's happenin' either . . . I reckon," Graham said.

We got to school and decided we would talk like cowboys the whole day. Everyone in our class had dressed up, except David. He punched me in the arm when I walked in and told me I looked like a dork. I don't know what got into me, but I punched him right back and said, "I reckon you shouldn't mess with old Tex." David gave me a strange look and backed up to his seat, without even another punch.

"Whoa, what was that all about?" Graham asked. "I've never seen David back off without getting in the last punch."

"I don't know. I think it's these cowboy clothes. They make me feel kind of tough or something,"

"Or kind of *manly*," Graham said. His eyes got big. "Hey, I think it's my manly coaching paying off."

"Good morning, students," Mrs. Gibson said. "You all look so festive today. Thank you for dressing up. David, I have an extra bandana you can wear." David looked mad but didn't say anything. "And everyone is here except Zach. I'm going to call his home to find out if he's going to be able to make it. But if he won't be here, Raymond, would you mind dancing with Heidi?"

"Would I ever!" I blurted out. Everyone turned and looked at me. Diane started laughing. "I mean . . . I . . . um, reckon that would be all right." I looked over at Graham, and he gave me a thumbs-up sign.

We spent the rest of the morning doing regular school stuff. We had a spelling test and did some math. For some reason everything was more fun, even schoolwork, when I was dressed as a cowboy. In no time at all, it was time to line up for lunch.

"What kind of grub do you reckon they're cookin' today?" I asked Graham on the way to the lunchroom.

"Would you two stop talking like that!" Lizzy said, interrupting our Western conversation.

"Well, I'm sorry, little lady, but I'm afraid that ain't possible," Graham said. "You see, we're cowboys and that's the way we talk."

"Then sit far away from me, because I can't stand to hear you anymore!" Lizzy whined.

"Sorry, ma'am. But we've been riding the range all morning and now it's time for some grub. If the lunchroom ain't big enough for the three of us, you may just have to find your own place to eat," I said.

She flipped her hair around and ignored us.

Pretty soon we got more of our friends to start talking with a Western accent, and before we knew it, almost everyone in our class was speaking like cowboys. Mrs. Gibson didn't even get mad when we spoke like that in class. She said she thought it was appropriate for the occasion.

As soon as Lizzy heard that, she started speaking with an accent. "Howdy, Mrs. Gibson," Lizzy said. "I think you're the best darn teacher in the West."

"Don't you mean, you 'reckon' she's the best darn teacher in the West?" Graham added. Everyone laughed . . . except Lizzy.

Finally, it was time for the performance. Mrs. Gibson told us how important it was to smile and keep dancing even if we made a mistake. We lined up and walked down to the auditorium. Mr. Fowl's class was ahead of us. They went straight onto the stage to sing. We waited in the hall next to our dance partners. We listened and waited for our turn.

"Raymond," Mrs. Gibson said. "Zach's mother said he wasn't feeling well this morning, but that he would try to make it. However, since he's not here yet, why don't you line up next to Heidi?"

I ran over and stood in Zach's place next to Heidi. I looked at her and smiled. "Howdy ma'am," I said. "I reckon I'm going to be dancing with you." Somehow this cowboy costume even made it easier to think of things to say to girls. I wondered if I could start wearing a cowboy costume every day or if people would think I was weird.

"I guess, if I have no other choice," she laughed.

Pretty soon the singing ended and we heard the audience clap. The backstage door opened and Mr. Fowl led his class into the hall. I looked back at Graham and saw his red hair poking out of the line. He was practicing dancing in place. Heidi looked at me and said, "Are you ready, cowboy?"

"Yep," I said. "I reckon I am." As I walked onto the stage next to Heidi, I thought about the manly rules. I hadn't cried, I had written a poem, I'd even talked to Heidi more than normal, and most importantly I was following rule number three: A man does whatever it takes to dance with his girl. Sure, I had a little help from Zach being absent, but it still counts.

Mrs. Gibson held the stage door open while we all marched in, two by two, and got into our places. I was on the side closest to where our parents were sitting. As I looked over to wave at my mom and dad, my heart suddenly sank. Zach was walking in with his mom. He was dressed up in his Western clothes. His mom walked him up onto the stage close to where I was standing. Since we were all in our places already, Mrs. Gibson told Zach to come up and dance with her in the front. I could hear him from where I stood.

"I can't, I feel too sick," he said.

Whew, I thought.

"Go on up, Zach," his mom told him. "That's why we're here."

"I really don't feel good," he said.

"That's okay, Zach," Mrs. Gibson said. Instead of being part of the dance, Mrs. Gibson walked to a free chair at the end of the front row and sat down.

"Zach, do you really feel sick?" his mom asked after Mrs. Gibson was gone.

"No, I just don't want to dance with the teacher," he said. "I won't do it."

I looked over at Mrs. Gibson. She was sitting by herself all dressed up in her Western clothes. They didn't look new. I figured they were probably the same clothes she wore dancing with her husband years ago. Then all of a sudden I did something I knew I would probably regret my whole life. I walked over to Zach and his mom, who had walked backstage.

"Zach, do you want your regular spot by Heidi?" I asked. He looked at me and then at his mom.

"Uh, yeah . . . if that's okay with you. Thanks!" He hurried out to my empty spot next to Heidi.

Maybe I just wasn't cut out to be a man yet. I guess manly rule number three would have to wait until I was older. I walked down the big stage steps and over to Mrs. Gibson. "Um, howdy ma'am, do you reckon I could have this dance?" I asked, holding my arm out.

She sat there silently for a moment, and when she looked up at me, her eyes were shining. "Why, that's mighty kind of you, cowboy," she said with a big wrinkly smile. She stood up and took my arm, and we walked up to our place in front of the group. Graham gave me an *are you crazy?* look as we passed by. I just smiled.

Right then the music started. I have to admit we all looked great. Everyone do-si-doed perfectly and bowed at all the right times. When the dance ended, the audience cheered and we all bowed again. It was a great moment. Mrs. Gibson bent down and put her wrinkly face close to mine.

"Thank you for dancing with an old lady with gray hair and huge glasses. You're a fine young man, Raymond," she said. Then she walked away to talk to some parents.

A chill went down my spine. She called me a fine young *man*! She didn't say "baby" or even "boy." She said *man*. As I stood there feeling good, Graham ran up to me.

"Well, pardner," he said. "That was pretty fun. We made it through our first dance. I reckon this makes us real dancin' dudes."

"I reckon you're right," I answered.

"And I don't know what got into you back there," Graham added. "You know, leaving Heidi to dance with Mrs. Gibson . . . but I have to admit that was mighty nice of you. And I reckon manly rule number six must be: Always do something nice for an old lady."

"Thanks, coach," I said. But he wasn't listening. "Graham?" I waved my hand in front of his face. He was staring at something over by the school doors. It was Kelly.

"I'd like to stay and chat," Graham said, his eyes

still focused on Kelly, "but I see a cowgirl over there all alone. I think I'll just mosey on over and see if I can interest her in one final do-si-do." He shuffled away like he was still dancing. I laughed as I turned to go find my parents.

"Whoa, sorry," I said, turning and bumping into someone. "Oh, hey, Heidi," I said. "Um . . . great dancing out there." I hoped I hadn't hurt her feelings by choosing to dance with Mrs. Gibson instead of her. "Sorry, Heidi, I really wanted to dance with you, and I hope you don't think—"

"Well, this is what I think," Heidi said, smiling. "I reckon you were just being a darn nice cowboy."

Suddenly I had a funny feeling inside. It was a good funny feeling. I smiled back at her. "Shoooot, little lady," I said, adjusting my cowboy hat farther back on my head. "That's awful kind of you. May I walk you to your horse?" I said. I held out my arm and we both laughed.

"Why, that would be mighty nice, cowboy," Heidi said, taking my arm, and together we walked into the sunset. Well, into the parking lot.

2) 6/13